T0117017

The Adventures of Emily and Bella the Horse

The Adventures of Emily and Bella the Horse

Emily and Bella Brave the Storm

by
Christine Robinson
Illustrated by Linda N. Chisholm

iUniverse, Inc.
Bloomington   New York

The Adventures of Emily and Bella the Horse
Emily and Bella Brave the Storm

iUniverse books may be ordered through booksellers or by contacting:

iUniverse
1663 Liberty Drive
Bloomington, IN 47403
www.iuniverse.com
1-800-Authors (1-800-288-4677)

Because of the dynamic nature of the Internet, any Web addresses or links contained in this book may have changed since publication and may no longer be valid. This is a work of fiction. All of the characters, names, incidents, organizations, and dialogue in this novel are either the products of the author's imagination or are used fictitiously.

ISBN: 978-1-4401-8176-4 (pbk)
ISBN: 978-1-4401-8177-1 (ebk)

Printed in the United States of America
iUniverse rev. date: 11/18/2009

Chapter 1
Bella

Bella was grazing in her pasture when a cool breeze ruffled her soft black mane. She lifted her head and looked to the north. In the distance, the flat black clouds of a storm swept across the Oregon sky. Storms like these had swept across the hills and mountains before, and Bella made her way toward her cozy stall and warm hay bedding.

Eleven-year-old Emily came out of the house with a handful of carrots. She could see Bella raise her head, could hear Bella's soft whinny calling to groom her. Emily called Bella's name and opened the gate. She could tell that Bella was happy to see her. Bella put her soft brown muzzle onto Emily's shoulder, and the smell of the sweet carrots and Bella's warm breath filled the air.

"C'mon, Bella, there's a storm, and you need to go into your stall," Emily said, pulling on Bella's mane. Emily was feeling impatient today because she had a particularly hard day at school, but being with Bella always calmed her nerves. Emily was just happy to have Bella with her.

"Bella, you have no idea what it's been like at school." Emily sighed heavily.

"Taylor tapped me on the shoulder to show me a funny drawing of the teacher, and when I looked, she raised her hand and said I was copying her test! I had to stay after class. I tried to explain what happened, but the teacher just shook her head and told me I would have to stay after class to do some extra work." Emily took a deep breath and Bella snorted. Emily always felt better after running her hands over Bella's shiny brown coat. Bella listened to Emily better than anyone she knew, including her family.

Emily took very good care of Bella, and in return, Bella was Emily's best friend. Even when Emily was in a bad mood, Bella could always lift her spirits. Emily would groom Bella for hours. Combing out Bella's mane and brushing her coat was her favorite chore. She could tell Bella liked it because Bella would close her eyes and cock a hip to rest while she brushed her. Emily loved scratching Bella's back with the grooming brushes. She almost never had a speck of mud on her from all the grooming she got.

Emily took great pride in seeing Bella cleaned and groomed. The judges always remarked on Bella's beautiful coat and mane when she competed. Emily always felt most at ease and accepted in the show ring.

When Bella got into the stall, Emily fed her three carrots. Bella nosed Emily's pocket to check if she was hiding any more goodies.

"Okay, Bella, you know I always save the best for last. Here's your apple."

When Bella bit into it, the juice squirted out and hit Emily in the face. She started laughing so hard she had to hold herself up around Bella's neck. Emily needed a good laugh especially after the rotten trick Taylor pulled on her. Sometimes after school, she would just come straight to Bella's pasture and sit with her. Sometimes she would cry about those terrible girls that made fun of her muddy boots or hay in her hair. They would call her names and ask if she slept in a stall.

There was one girl, Taylor Carey, that would whinny at her and tell her she smelled like manure. Emily knew that Taylor had a very expensive and well-bred horse, but her horse couldn't compare to Bella.

Taylor made fun of her every chance she got because she was jealous that her horse didn't care about her at all. Taylor was also jealous that Emily won blue ribbons on Bella and Taylor was always coming in second place, no matter what horse she brought to the shows. Taylor was always trying to be the center of attention.

"Taylor might have the most expensive horse, but she doesn't have you," Emily said. Bella whinnied at Emily. "She never gives her horses the chance to shine, and she is so impatient. She must have gone through five horses this show season. She never builds trust with her horses, and they never trust her. Hard to win blue ribbons when you forget what horse you're riding that day." Emily laughed, and the bitterness of the day started to fade away.

"Actually, Bella. I sort of feel sorry for her. I don't

think she has a friend to talk to like I do." Emily leaned forward to kiss Bella's nose.

Emily and Bella had a very special friendship built on trust and mutual respect. Ever since Bella was born, Emily had been there with her. Emily was a very little girl when her mom first took her to the stall to see the newborn foal, *and* Emily was the first person to ever touch Bella. Since the moment they saw each other, they were inseparable. Emily's thoughts faded from Bella and back to Taylor.

Taylor wore makeup and always talked about which boy she liked. Emily tried to bite her tongue, but some days, Taylor and her clique of friends were just darn right mean!

Emily didn't care about boys and makeup. She liked her horse, and she liked to be outside. Emily knew that some of the other girls didn't want to join in the name-calling, but they were afraid to stand up to Taylor. Emily always just tried to ignore them. Even when she felt like crying, Emily just thought about Bella and how she was waiting for her to get home.

Emily was lost in thought about the day at school when she heard the first rumble of thunder. It was so loud it shook the barn and made Emily jump.

"Wow, that scared me. I guess I was thinking about school again. Well, Bella, you'll be safe here tonight. See you in the morning."

With that, Emily turned out the barn lights and left Bella to doze and eat hay in the dry stall.

Chapter 2
The Storm Begins

The rain fell hard on Bella's roof all night. The fierce wind whipped through the center aisle of the barn, tossing buckets and tack onto the floor. Emily was worried about Bella, but she knew that the barn was the safest place for Bella to be.

When Emily woke that morning, she overheard her dad talking about some cows that had broke loose in the storm. She made up her mind that she was going to do something useful and help her dad and brother. She was always getting left behind because she was the baby of the family.

"Well, not today, Emily Harris! You are going to go tell your dad you are going!"

She also heard them say that the cows had gone down into the valley, and she had never gone to the valley before, even when she went on rides with her brother. Her dad always told her to stick to the trails close to home for safety. When she asked her dad if she could help round up the cows, his eyes grew big with surprise.

"Honey," he said, "those cows have been spooked, and we have at least a hundred head out there. I've got to take a couple men and Jason. I don't want to be worried about you getting run over by some cow that doesn't know where she's going or why she's going there."

"Dad, I can help, and Bella is a good horse that knows her way around. Let me go with. Please!"

"Em, I'm sorry, but I'm not taking you this time. The storm is supposed to pick up again later this morning, and I don't want you to get caught in it and be miserable."

She looked at her brother with pleading eyes, but he only shrugged his shoulders. He really couldn't plead her case anyway. When Dad said something, the Harris family just did it—no questions asked. But Emily was feeling particularly frustrated that her dad still treated her like a little kid.

"Why? Why can't I go?" Emily questioned. "When are you going to let me help?"

"Emily, I've got to get to work. Jason, let's go."

Emily's dad and brother walked out of the house, leaving Emily standing in the kitchen.

"Well, I'm going," Emily said under her breath.

"Emily Ann!" her mom called, "I've got some things I need you to do this morning."

"But Mom, I've gotta let Bella out." Emily knew that Bella's breakfast was long past due. She could hear Bella's loud whinny and knew Bella was growing impatient.

"Bella can wait. It's raining, and it won't hurt her to stay inside for a few hours this morning."

"Fine, but I'm still going for a ride today," Emily said, her voice full of frustration. Her mom just gave her a look that told her she better watch it or she wouldn't be riding for a week. Emily didn't want that to happen because riding Bella was the only thing she ever wanted to do. If Emily couldn't ride Bella then Emily would sit for hours just watching Bella run around and stretch her legs in the pasture. Sometimes Bella would stand on a little hill in the pasture and graze, and sometimes Emily would stand with Bella on that hill and look at the whole valley below her.

After a long rain, the air was clear and fresh, and Emily could smell the wet earth beneath her boots. She loved to look at the hoofprints Bella left in the mud.

Emily changed her attitude and asked what needed done. The quicker she did her chores, the quicker she could get on her way.

After she finished the housework, Emily started packing her saddlebags. She wanted to make sure she had packed all the things she thought might be useful, including rope, water, a first aid kit, a hoof pick, and a cell phone.

Finally, Emily made it out to the barn to let Bella out.

Chapter 3
Emily Gets Bella

Emily popped her head up and around the corner of Bella's stall.

"Sorry, Bell, the storm is causing an awful mess, and the cattle got scattered to the four winds. Daddy has been out all morning rounding up strays, and Mom had me in all morning doing chores. I never want to see another dirty dish again!" Emily laughed as she got out the grooming tray and a couple of flakes of hay. She put the hay in the feeder and started to brush Bella's long black tail and mane.

"I didn't sleep very well because of the thunder and wind. I was kind of scared! I hope you slept better," she said as she started brushing Bella's soft brown coat with the finishing brush. "At least it's Saturday, and I don't have to go to school."

"I think it's time we saddle up and help Dad find the cattle. The thunder always makes them nervous and jumpy. What do you think, Bella? Are you up for a ride?" Emily always enjoyed rides on her best friend's back; they would often go down by the pond or on a long meandering trail that looped around the house on the mountainside. But this would be a new adventure.

Emily had taken Bella to help round up cattle before, but she mostly just watched and sat on the edge of the pasture. Emily's dad would do most of the work on his tough cow horses. The cow horses were usually kept in the lower pasture so Emily could get to Bella without fighting the herd. Bella was kept in her own little pasture with the hill, and Emily liked it that way. She never had to fight to get to her, and she was able to spend a lot of extra time with just her.

Emily got a riding saddle out and put it on Bella's back. Bella was a little horse, but she was very strong and powerful. Emily was tall, light, and a very good rider, so Bella carried her with ease. Emily was well-balanced, and even when Bella had to curve around a tight fence post or canter up a hill, Emily was never scared and was always confident.

Emily trusted Bella, and Bella trusted Emily. Emily cinched up Bella and put the bit in her mouth. She led her through the little gate and down a little hill that went to the driveway where Emily always mounted up, and Bella stood as still as a statue and waited for Emily to settle into the saddle.

Emily turned around in the saddle to check her saddlebags, and she glanced up to see her mom waving from the ranch house window. There was a coolness to the summer air, and Emily was excited and nervous. Her mom came out of the house.

"Emily, where are you going?"

"Umm, I haven't made up my mind yet, Mom, but I'll probably be gone for the rest of the day, okay?" Emily crossed her fingers behind her back and hoped her mom would just let her leave without having to tell her she was going into the valley.

"Well, be careful, you have your phone?"

"Yes, Mom, I have it. Bye!"

"Stay close to home. Your dad says the weather is supposed to get worse"

"Bye, Mom, bye"

"All right, Bella, you ready to go? Dad said the cows went down into the valley this morning, so let's go that way." With that, Emily gave a little kick and a click of her tongue, and Bella knew it was time to go.

Chapter 4
Down into the Valley

It was late morning and the storm had let up. There was just the after rain moisture hanging in the air. Emily was excited and a little nervous—they were going down into the valley. Emily had never defied her father before, and at least her mom didn't make her tell her where she was going. Emily pointed Bella south, and they started on their journey.

It was quiet and peaceful. Emily could see the low black clouds pushed up on the mountainside and wondered if the storm was over. There was a gentle breeze, and she could smell the earth with every step Bella took. They traveled down past the grove of pine trees and past the pear orchards. Emily thought that it looked like someone had rolled out green carpet in between the rows of pear trees. She saw a doe resting on the soft green grass. Bella saw it too, but the doe just stayed put, not wanting to leave its comfortable bed.

Emily settled into the saddle. The quietness of the

trail made Emily thoughtful, and she started to talk to Bella about all the trouble at school. "Bella, that girl, Taylor, makes me so mad. Sometimes I want to pull all her hair out and call her names."

Emily sighed heavily. She was feeling very angry and sad at the same time. "I just don't know what else I can do. Mom tells me to ignore her, but it's kind of hard when she is yelling names at me across the hall. It feels like the whole school is looking at me. Sometimes I wish I could fight back. I'm scared though. What if I got expelled from school? Mom might just be mad enough to take you away from me. I can't let Taylor get to me."

Bella continued to walk along the path that would eventually lead them down into the valley. Emily continued to let her troubles with Taylor tumble out.

"Mom just doesn't understand how horrible it is at school. I don't have any friends. The couple of girls I talk to just pretend like they don't know me when Taylor comes around. I don't blame them though. Taylor is probably the meanest girl at school, and no one wants her to pick on them."

Emily felt better telling Bella all of her troubles. Just the motion of her swaying horse and the breezy morning started to lift Emily's spirit even though her heart was heavy with sadness. Last week, Taylor was particularly cruel to Emily.

"Taylor is just mad that I won the blue ribbon in gymkhana. She didn't even place! She's just mad that she lost and we won Bella. That's why she calls us names."

Taylor taunted Emily all Friday morning. She even called Bella nothing but a cow with hay between her ears. Emily was so angry she ran from Taylor and her friends.

"I can't believe I let Taylor get to me. Mom was mad I left school, but after I told her what happened, she covered for me."

Emily thought she didn't need to compete on Bella anymore if it meant Taylor would leave her alone. Maybe that would help keep Taylor from being so mean. It always seemed that after a weekend of competition, the taunts were the worst.

Emily knew that her mom wanted to help her but didn't know how. She knew that her mom was just hoping things would work themselves out, but Emily didn't think they ever would.

Chapter 5
Emily Sings

The landscape was gradually changing into a mixture of forest and meadows that were mostly occupied by deer, ground squirrels, skunks, and raccoons. Bella was walking on a well-worn deer path when Emily started singing a song about all the pretty horses.

Hush-a-bye, don't you cry,
Go to sleep-y, little baby.
When you wake, you shall have
All the pretty little horses:
Blacks and bays, dapple grays,
Coach and six white horses.
Hush-a-bye, don't you cry,
Go to sleep-y little baby.

This was Em's favorite lullaby, and her voice was so beautiful that even the birds stopped to listen. As she sang, Emily relaxed. Singing helped distract her from thinking about school.

Soon the wind picked up, and the leaves rustled around Bella's legs. Emily stopped singing and grew more tense as the wind blew harder. Realizing the storm was not over, Emily remembered she didn't bring a raincoat.

"At least I have my helmet," she thought.

Emily knew that her nervousness made Bella nervous, so she tried to relax as best she could. They were riding into an area Emily had never been, but she kept Bella moving forward. The wind made Bella's mane stand straight up, and Emily reached forward to smooth it down again.

There were a lot of broken branches from the storm, and Emily was worried that Bella might trip or hit her legs on the rough bark of the fallen saplings. Emily could feel Bella lifting her feet high when she stepped over the fallen trees, and she never once hit her hooves when going across them. Emily was glad she had such an agile horse.

Emily had been riding for a couple of hours straight into the valley. During the ride, Emily couldn't keep her thoughts from going back to her dilemma at school. How was she going to get through the sixth grade? Taylor made it so miserable for her that she thought of elaborate plans that would keep her out of school for the whole year. She thought maybe if she got sick or her family moved to Alaska, she would not have to face Taylor and her friends ever again, but she knew that wasn't going to happen any time soon. If she got sick, who would take care of Bella? If they moved, where would Bella go?

Her thoughts were deep, and Emily almost forgot the task at hand, but she was interrupted by shouts coming from the edge of the thick strand of trees. Emily sat straight up. "Do you hear that, Bella?"

They headed straight for cries of "help me!" Emily urged Bella forward quickly, and they soon found themselves facing a swollen stream filled with the previous night's rain. Crying and sitting on the other side of the stream calling for help was—of all people—Taylor.

Chapter 6
Emily Finds Taylor

"Emily, help me! I'm hurt, and I can't get up!" Taylor's pain-filled eyes met Emily's across the stream. Emily was so surprised to see anyone out there, let alone her worst enemy, that she completely forgot what she had come down to the valley for. Emily knew that she had to get to Taylor and help her though, even if she was the meanest girl she knew. Emily saw there was no way she could get Bella across the stream. It was moving too quickly and would knock Bella over. There were also a lot of fast-moving sticks and debris in the water. Emily was scared and wondering what Taylor was doing out in the middle of the woods. Emily yelled across the stream, "I've got to find a better place to cross! Don't move!"

"Well, Bella, we need to find a spot that we can cross. Let's head downstream." They picked their way downstream, over the rocks and branches. The wind was getting stronger, and the branches on the trees waved. The creek seemed to be getting wider as they went downstream, but Emily was determined to get to Taylor and help her.

Bella's ears were straight up. Emily did not like that the wind was blowing so hard, and then the first sprinkling of rain started to come down. The thunder was like someone starting a big motorcycle, and the lightning was flashing just as fast as the thunder rumbled.

Her dad had said that there was just a lull in the storm, but the weather was supposed to get worse. Dad said more rain was headed to the valley all day. It made her very worried, and she thought she might not find her way back if it got too bad. As if finding Taylor hurt wasn't enough, a skunk popped out of the brush. Bella was usually a very calm horse, but this caught her off guard, and she sidestepped right into the rushing creek and started to lose her footing.

Chapter 7
Bella and Emily Cross the Stream

Fortunately, Emily kept her balance while Bella was looking for firm footing. They were on the bank of the creek, and the loose stones and pebbles made it hard for Bella to stand still. Emily made the decision to cross the stream right there.

"Well, we're already wet, and it looks shallow enough to cross. Let's go!"

Emily wasn't sure about that decision, but she trusted Bella could make it, so she urged Bella slowly across the stream. The water was so cold it made Emily's legs numb. She could feel Bella slipping on the rounded rocks below. Emily hoped both she and Bella would be able to move across the stream without falling.

The rushing water was strong, and as Emily urged her forward, Bella tripped on a big rock. Both Emily and Bella went into the stream, but Bella regained her footing, and Emily kept a tight grip on Bella's mane. Emily walked next to Bella, and all Emily could think about was holding on.

They were almost across when Emily fell again. She was soaked from head to toe, but she got to the creek bank by clawing her way through the pebbles, stones, and mud. Bella managed to move over toward where Emily lay. The rain started to come down harder, and it washed over Emily's helmet like a waterfall. Emily was scared, but she knew Bella would not leave her. Emily didn't move. She just lay still, glad that she was on the other side.

Emily was numb with cold. Bella put her soft brown nose on the back of Emily's neck. That's when Emily rolled over crying and reaching for Bella's mane to pull herself up. "We did it! We made it across the creek. Now we just have to find our way back to Taylor."

The rain came in driving sheets. Emily started to cry harder. Holding on to Bella's neck, she cried, "What are we going to do! I didn't tell anyone where we were going, and I'm not even sure I know how to get back. How can I get both Taylor and me back? I don't even know where Taylor is anymore."

Emily could only lean up against Bella as she tried to regain her strength and get some warmth from her friend and companion. Emily looked right into Bella's bright brown eyes and knew then that it wouldn't be Emily getting them back, it would be Bella. Emily knew

Bella could get her back safely, but she still wasn't sure she could also help Taylor. Emily was cold, wet, and muddy.

"Bella, we should just go home. I can tell Taylor we will go for help. Why should I help her anyway?"

Chapter 8
Emily Thinks Twice about Helping Taylor

"Taylor was never once nice to me. It would have been easier if she just ignored me." Emily was exasperated. The one person who she didn't want to see was asking her for help.

Emily buried her face into Bella's wet, soft neck, and Bella nudged Emily toward the saddle, willing her to get back on so they could get going. Emily thought about how scared she would be if she were hurt and didn't have Bella with her. They were across the river now, but they had traveled much farther downstream than either of them had wanted.

Soaked and tired, Emily got back up on Bella's back and reached into the saddlebags she had packed and pulled out some apples and water. She reached down and gave Bella an apple. "You are such a good horse."

Emily decided right there that she wasn't mean, even

if Taylor was. Emily was going to help. She hoped that the person that found her would help if she was ever lost and hurt. "Come on, Bella, we have work to do."

At that point, Emily remembered the cell phone she brought in case of an emergency. "Well, this is an emergency!" Emily reached into the saddlebag and pulled out a thoroughly soaked cell phone. When Emily opened it up, she could see that it had been ruined by the water and the pounding it got from the rocks.

Emily was on the verge of crying again, but deep inside, she knew it was up to her to help Taylor. So she sat up in the saddle and urged Bella upstream to where they last saw Taylor.

Chapter 9
Taylor

Emily carefully made her way upstream with Bella. She had hoped she wouldn't have to travel too far downstream, but the rain swelled the creek past its banks in some places. When Bella was spooked into the water, Emily thought she was going too far. So Taylor had to be at least fifteen minutes travel time on Bella. Emily was careful to try and guide Bella away from the stones of the creek because they were slippery and hard on Bella's hooves.

She found an animal trail a few feet from the stream that was wide enough for her and Bella to walk on.

"Come on, Bella. This trail should make things a little easier."

After about ten minutes of slowly moving up the trail, Emily could hear Taylor crying. Emily guided Bella toward her and came up to a terrible sight. Taylor was dirty, and her face was scratched. She was covered in the soft mud from the stream, and she was holding her left ankle.

"Emily!" Taylor cried. "I thought you were going to leave me here!"

"Why would you think that?" Emily asked. "I'm not like you, Taylor. I actually care about people."

Emily's eyes narrowed, not knowing what horrible things Taylor might say to her. After sliding off Bella's back, Emily walked over to Taylor. "What happened, Taylor, and why are you out here?"

Emily could see she must have been here for a while. Taylor's usual perfect appearance was less than perfect with mascara running down her face and red splotches on her cheeks from crying. Her eyes were red and glassy.

"I took Chance out for a ride this morning," Taylor explained. "I wanted to go somewhere new, so I started down into the valley. We were going along just fine for a couple of hours when a branch broke practically right on top of us. He took off running. I held on for as long as I could, but he was running so fast!"

Taylor started crying again. "He almost killed me, Emily! I held on, thinking he would eventually stop, but when we got to this creek, he thought he could jump over it! He made it about halfway, and the creek slowed him down, so I jumped off and landed on these rocks. I hurt my ankle really bad. Emily, you have to help me!"

Chapter 10
Emily and Taylor

"Taylor, we have at least a three-hour ride home. Do you want me to go back as fast as I can and get help?"

"Don't leave me!" Taylor cried out. "I would be so scared to wait. I can ride; I just can't walk. My ankle is the only place that's hurt. Do you think Bella can take us?" Emily knew Bella could take them. "Yes, Bella can take us. We can't cross the stream here though; it's too fast, and there are too many sticks and logs in the water for Bella to get us across. Let's get you off the ground. We'll figure out a way back with Bella's help."

Emily reached down for Taylor's hand and pulled her up. Emily helped Taylor hop over to a dozing Bella. While Emily was fixing Bella's saddle, she heard Taylor whisper in Bella's ear, "I wish I had a horse like you." A little smile formed at the corner of Emily's mouth. She finally knew the truth: Taylor never had a friend that would stay with her no matter what happened, a friend to stick by her.

Emily decided right there that she had made the right decision to help Taylor. Emily tightened the saddle and came around to help Taylor up. "You ride in back, Taylor." Emily gave Taylor a leg up, and then she mounted up. Bella shifted her weight to accommodate both riders, and then Emily gently urged Bella back to the animal trail alongside the stream.

Emily could feel Taylor start to relax with the swaying of Bella's walk, although she could still hear Taylor sniffle a little from crying so hard and being wet and cold. The rain continued, but it was gentle, and there was no wind.

After several minutes of riding, Taylor asked, "Emily, what were you doing in the valley this morning?"

Emily said, "I wanted to prove to my dad that I could help around the ranch. The cows broke free last night, and I wanted to go. My dad told me that he didn't want me to round up cows because he thought I would get hurt, especially in the storm. Jason and Dad left a few hours before me though, so I don't know what direction they went. Bella and I just went down and we found you." Emily started to laugh a little. "Weird. Huh?" Taylor agreed. Emily could feel that Taylor was starting to recover, and Emily asked, "How are you feeling?"

"I'm just glad those cows got out and you were stubborn enough to go look for them. I'm ... I'm ... sorry, Emily. Sorry that I've been so mean. And just so you know, I think Bella is an amazing horse. How do you guys win every time you compete? I have the best horses in the county, and I still can't beat you."

Emily smiled to herself and realized that Taylor was envious of her and Bella. Emily thought about that for a minute and replied, "We don't go in to win. We go because we love to play! Bella is my best friend, and we just like to be together."

Emily could tell that Taylor was surprised she didn't go to competition just to show Taylor what a great horse Bella was and to win. Emily thought that maybe now that Taylor knew she was there to be with Bella and not to beat Taylor, she might just stop her taunts.

Emily was starting to lose her grudge against Taylor. In fact, she thought maybe they might become good enough friends that they could ride together.

Taylor interrupted Emily's thoughts by asking, "Do you think the cows are much farther into the valley? I could help you look if you don't think it would be too hard on Bella to keep carrying both of us."

"I don't know, Taylor. We should get you home," Emily said, although she couldn't help wondering about the cows and how her dad didn't think she could help. "Well, we have to find a safe place to cross, so we'll keep our eyes out for any strays while we're looking for a way back home," Taylor said.

Emily nodded in agreement as the rain continued down on both girls.

Chapter 11
Trying to Get Home

"It's past lunchtime, fortunately I told my mom I was going to be gone most of the afternoon," Emily said to Taylor. Emily pointed Bella upstream to try and make her way back to a safe crossing.

Emily, Taylor, and Bella went over rocks and broken branches, and the rain continued to fall. At first it fell softly, but then it became a steady downpour. Emily was becoming increasingly worried. Where should she cross? It seemed as if the stream just kept getting wider. Would she be able to find her way back? Would Taylor be able to ride all the way home? She was worried Taylor might have broken her ankle. She thought maybe she should stop wondering about the cows and concentrate solely on getting Taylor home.

"Riding Bella is like sitting on a couch that moves," Emily told Taylor. "She is easy to sit back and relax on," Taylor nodded her head in agreement.

"She does move very smoothly. It feels like I'm home. Where's the popcorn?" Taylor and Emily laughed. Emily was happy Taylor was comfortable.

"How's your ankle feeling?" Emily asked

"It's throbbing a lot. I'm just glad I'm not walking. We should go home."

"It is going to take some time to get home. I'm just not sure how to get across this stream. It just seems to be getting wider the farther we go. I know it took a few hours to get to the stream where I found you, and now depending on if we get across, it will take a few hours to get home. Just try to relax. I have some food in my saddlebags if you're hungry."

The darkness of the storm clouds made it feel even later than it was and more like dusk. Emily was trying to figure out what to do next. They had been walking up the trail for at least half an hour. Emily definitely didn't want to swim across again, and it was getting colder. Her wet clothes stuck to her, and she was getting very uncomfortable.

Emily was starting to lose hope and thought maybe they were lost when Taylor said, "Emily, we're lost, and I'm cold and scared. My ankle hurts a lot too. We aren't going to get home tonight, are we?"

That was when Emily realized she had been giving Bella directions. Emily had been pulling the reins to the right, pointing Bella toward the stream. Emily was worried about losing sight of the stream. She was not giving Bella her head, and her reins were tight against Bella's mouth. Emily knew she was feeling nervous because she never rode with such tension in her arms. So as not to give away her nervousness to Taylor, Emily said in a very calm voice,

"Bella, take us home." Then Emily dropped her hands and the reins and gave Bella her head. Bella veered to the left away from the stream and into an open field.

"What are you doing, Emily?" Taylor cried. Before Emily could stop her, Taylor grabbed the reins and yanked on Bella hard to the right.

"We have to stay near the creek!" When Taylor yanked, Bella spun hard to the right and Taylor fell to the ground.

"Don't you ever do that—ever! I should just leave you here, Taylor Carey. You're mean, and you never trust anyone or anything. That's your problem. Bella will get us home. It might not be tonight, but it will happen. I trust her."

Taylor started to cry. "Emily, I want to go home. I thought we could look for the cows, but my ankle is hurting, and I'm cold and hungry." Taylor started to cry harder.

"I told you to get some food out of the saddlebags." Emily yelled, "Bella will get us home if you just trust her. Maybe if you trusted your horses more they would give you more. You're selfish and mean, and your friends are only your friends because they're scared of you. Well I'm not scared of you, Taylor, and that's why you pick on me. I'm not scared; I feel sorry for you because you never had anyone or anything care about you back. I should just leave you and get my parents."

"Emily, no!" Taylor whined. "I'm sorry. Please let me back up; I won't do it again. I trust you and Bella. I'm sorry. Don't leave."

Emily thought about what Taylor did. Emily didn't want Bella to get hurt or frightened, but she couldn't just leave Taylor. The later it got, the more Emily thought about shelter for the night. Even though it was midafternoon, Emily wasn't sure she could get Taylor back. Home seemed very far away. Emily wasn't too worried about having to stay out for the night, but she was worried about Taylor. She was also tired of being wet. She would have to find shelter before it got too late.

"Taylor, I'm sorry you're hurt, but this isn't any easier for me or my horse. Bella wants to go the opposite direction that I want to go. I know home is across the stream and toward those hills. I have no idea why she went away from the stream, but I trust Bella to get me where I need to go and you need to trust her too."

For the first time Emily thought that maybe Bella wasn't going to take them home. Maybe Emily put too much faith in Bella. Emily's thoughts were interrupted by a rustling in the tall grass. "Taylor, be quiet. There's something in the meadow."

"What? What is it? Help me up, Emily, I'm scared."

"Be quiet," Emily whispered harshly. She scanned the open space for the animal that was rustling the grass, at the far edge of the meadow. She started to think about her dad. She knew her dad would be angry at her for coming into the valley to look for cows when he told her not to. Now she wished he was here. What if it was a bear or cougar? She was terrified at what she would find. She would be in trouble, but she didn't think it would be this hard to find a cow, and now she wasn't sure what Bella found for her.

Chapter 12
Bella Finds What Emily Was Looking For

Emily realized the rustling of the grass came from the tree line on the far side of the field. She could also hear a low mooing. Emily was happy and excited. It wasn't a bear or cougar but cows!

"Taylor, stay put. I think we found what I came out here to find in the first place." "Cows! Bella found the cows!" Taylor was excited and crying at the same time.

Emily yelled over her shoulder, "Stay put! I'll be back for you."

Emily headed across the meadow, through the tall grass. Emily was glad Bella was so surefooted. She relaxed into the saddle and tried not to think about her stomach rumbling.

"Well, what do you think, Bella? How many cows do you think are over there?"

Bella lifted her head and smelled the air.

"You knew exactly where you were going the whole time, didn't you, girl?"

Bella expertly weaved around stumps and rocks, trees and puddles. Emily was always careful to keep the creek in earshot so she would not get lost. She also saw that Taylor had fallen by a huge cedar that she could pick out from anywhere in the field. Emily was definitely farther away from home than she had ever been, but she was beginning to have reasonable assurance that she would at least get home because Bella could get her there. Bella knew exactly what she was doing.

Bella kept popping up her head. Emily was sure Bella smelled something that reminded her of home. Emily pointed Bella in the direction of the cattle. She was concerned that she would get turned around and lose Taylor. Emily could hear the creek, but she had wound around a small knoll at the far side of the pasture. It obscured her view of the big cedar, but she could see the top of it. Emily tried to pull Bella back around the knoll.

"Come on, Bella. I don't want to get lost."

Bella just kept moving forward, away from the

stream and away from Taylor. Bella fought Emily all the way to the edge of the tree line. When they got all the way across the field, Emily could see that there was another small clearing and a lot more movement in the tall grass.

Bella stopped.

Emily was concerned about how many cattle they would find there. Bella whinnied and started moving forward, sure of what she saw and smelled. As they got closer, they could see a baby calf lying perfectly still in the small clearing, surrounded by a few other cows. Its eyes were bright and brown. The calf was staring intently at Bella and Emily, wondering if it should get up and move or stay put. Emily couldn't help but get excited.

"Bella, you did it! You found the cows!"

Emily was so happy. She realized that this was the same baby cow that her dad talked about a few days before. Her dad said one of the cows gave birth to a black-and-white calf in the field. This small band of cattle must have separated from the main herd. Emily knew they were the cows they were looking for because they had the Harris Ranch brand on their side.

Emily jumped off Bella and walked over to the baby

cow. She saw the momma cow grazing just behind the baby. The momma cow lifted her head up and gave a long and low moo. "Well now that we've found them, how am I going to get the cows and Taylor home?" Emily thought to herself.

She knew enough about cows that if she could get the momma to start heading toward home the baby would follow her. When Emily moved toward the calf, it sprang to its feet.

"Well, little cow, you definitely can move quick." Emily noticed that the calf had four white socks and a white stripe almost all the way around the middle of her black body. It reminded Emily of an Oreo cookie, so she decided to name the baby cow Oreo. She was so cute and looked so soft. Oreo's soft black nose sniffed at the air. Emily knew it was time to head home.

Chapter 13
Finding the Cows

Bella grazed contentedly in the little meadow while Emily looked at the calf. The rain had stopped, and the clouds were breaking up. The sun was peeking through the clouds. Emily knew that she had about four hours before it would get dark. That made her very nervous because she estimated that she was about three hours away from home, if she got back across the stream safely. She wanted to at least get the cattle and Taylor back across the creek before dark. They could find shelter on the other side of the creek and wait until morning if they had to. Emily was sure that her mom and dad would look for her. She was also sure that her dad would be furious. She didn't care though. In fact, even if her dad was mad, she wished he was with her now.

"Dad would come down toward the creek to find us for sure," Emily thought.

Emily was worried the baby wouldn't have enough strength to get across the creek, so Emily needed to get her roped before they tried to cross. If she could get the mom and Bella to cross together, Emily was certain she could handle Oreo.

"If I tie the rope to Bella's saddle, then if Oreo falls, Bella can help pull her up," Emily told herself. She hoped that Bella would be able to handle the extra weight if the calf fell in the water.

"Right now, I need to get the cattle across the meadow to the big cedar tree where I left Taylor."

Emily got up on Bella's back. She was glad that the rain had stopped. Emily wanted to make it home tonight.

"Okay, Bella, I promise you a nice big bucket of grain and beet pulp tonight if you get us home. I'll also throw in a bunch of carrots and a dry stall. We need to find a better place to cross the stream." Emily pleaded with Bella.

The more Emily thought about home, the more she was eager to get going, but Emily couldn't forget the creek and the trouble getting across. She now had four cows and Taylor.

"I know your hooves are going to be sore tomorrow from the rocks near the creek, Bella. I'm sorry but we have more work to do. Let's go."

Chapter 14
Going Home

Emily gave Bella a little kiss, and Bella knew it was time to go. Emily pointed Bella toward the momma cow, and they weaved their way over to her. She saw Bella coming and started to walk forward. Oreo wasn't sure what was happening, but she did know that her momma was walking away, so she was quick to follow. The rest of the cows followed as well. Bella was relaxed and Emily was glad she had such a versatile horse under her. Bella was driving them toward the stream when it started to rain again. "Well, it might be raining, but we're on our way home, Bella."

Bella and Emily got Oreo and the rest of the cattle to the edge of the clearing. Emily saw Taylor waving her arms as they got closer to the cedar tree. "You got them, Emily. Oh and there's a baby!"

"Taylor, I'm going to tell you right now that Bella's gotta get us home, so you just sit back and be glad you're not spending the night out here alone!"

"I promise." Then Taylor hopped over to Bella and put her arms around her neck. "Just get us home, girl, I trust you."

Emily got down and helped Taylor back up on Bella's back before getting back up herself.

"Thanks for not leaving me," Taylor whispered.

Emily smiled and said, "No problem, but next time I will!"

Taylor held on tight to Emily and didn't say another word. Emily could tell that Taylor was starting to appreciate Emily's toughness. Emily, it seemed, was the only one that was sticking by Taylor no matter what.

Emily started to ride toward the small herd, and as they got closer, she realized she had spent so much of her time trying to get Bella to follow the creek, she didn't notice any landmarks where they actually came out of the brush. The big tree was where Taylor fell off, not where they came out. Emily could hear the creek and saw the momma cow and the rest of the herd already walking down a path toward it. Emily was getting very tired and figured that path was good as any. Taylor just held on, and Emily dropped the reins and said, "Take us home, Bella. Take us home."

As they followed Oreo and Momma cow, Emily was

thinking about how beautiful it was in the valley. It was so quiet, and under the canopy of trees, she couldn't tell if it was still raining. She whispered in Bella's ear, "When the weather clears up, we're coming back. We'll get to know this area as good as we know the hills around the house." Bella nickered her approval of more adventures with Emily.

When they got to the creek, Emily could see that Momma cow had definitely gone a different way than they had when they first crossed the creek. Emily could see the creek, but they were on a creek bank that was soft with dark mud. There was a small waterfall that fell into a deep, dark pool. She could see that up the creek, just before the waterfall, there was a shallow sandbar. It went all the way across the creek, and the water was not so deep that it would pull Oreo under.

Emily had to get the herd to cross there. She felt so grateful that they found a place they could cross safely. Emily encouraged Bella to the shallow sandbar and started up the creek in the soft mud. Momma cow and Oreo were just behind them now on the edge of the bank. The rest of the cows were in front of them going upstream. Emily wasn't sure how she was going to get the cows across. In fact, Emily could feel Bella sinking deeper in the mud with each step, and with every step she sunk, Taylor's grip tightened around Emily's middle.

Emily was trying to move Bella to the side where the mud was not as thick. She could feel Bella picking her feet up as fast as she put them down. Her walk turned into a trot. Emily didn't think it would be a good idea to try and get the cows to cross through the mud, but as far as she could see, the sandbar was the best place to cross.

"Bella, we have to get the cows up the stream a little farther so they don't have to walk in the mud. Momma cow won't go through this with Oreo. Hold on, Taylor!"

Emily spun Bella around and they made their way back to where Momma cow, Oreo, and the others were standing. Oreo's bright eyes shined with this adventure. Emily knew that Oreo had to have walked across this stream once to get to the meadow they were in.

"Taylor, I think this must have been where the cattle crossed before. It's shallow enough and they seem to know where they are going."

Emily was afraid that the cattle would charge back to the little clearing and this would have just been a failed attempt. Emily felt confident that if she could get the cows and Bella to cross there, they would be able to make it home.

Emily could see Oreo was scared of the water and hid behind her mother. Emily brought Bella up behind Momma cow and Oreo. There was a little deer path that followed the creek up to the waterfall, and Bella nosed the cattle in that direction. The four cows stood still at the water's edge.

The cattle started to get nervous, and Oreo was waiting for her mother. Emily could see that Momma cow wasn't going to go across; she wanted to go back to the little meadow and graze. She tried to turn around, but Bella ran into her, pushing her into the creek.

"Oh no, Bella, I didn't rope Oreo yet! I need to get that rope around her so she doesn't get separated."

It was too late for Emily to safely rope Oreo, and Taylor holding her middle so tight Emily could barely breathe. "Taylor, let go of me a little! I can't breathe."

Taylor loosened her grip but was so scared she didn't say a word. Emily thought the shallow sandbar would be safe and Oreo wouldn't be so stressed if she could just follow her momma. Emily crossed her fingers and hoped Oreo would follow. Oreo wasn't too sure about the rushing water and didn't follow right away. In fact, Momma cow and the others were already across the creek before Oreo had even put her front hooves in.

"Come on, Oreo!" Emily yelled over the sound of the rushing stream. Emily was happy to have made it safely across, but Oreo was still on the wrong side of the creek. Emily could feel Taylor lean to the side to see what was going on.

Taylor started to speak. "Come on, Oreo. You can do it!"

It was the first time Emily ever heard Taylor encourage anyone or anything. Momma cow stopped on the edge of the creek bank and bellowed to her calf while the other two cows went into the brush ahead of them. Emily and Taylor could see Oreo was scared. She was weaving back and forth in front of the water's edge, and she was separated from her momma. Emily could see the baby cow wanted her mother so bad. Emily knew that Oreo saw the horse and the other cattle go across, so Emily kept her fingers crossed that Oreo would follow.

Oreo put in her front two hooves and then jumped back out before springing across the creek in short hops. Emily started to laugh. Taylor was clapping, and when Oreo got across the creek, Taylor hugged Emily. Emily was so happy that Oreo was brave enough to get across the creek. Oreo made it to the bank safely and pushed herself up against her mom. Finally across the creek, Emily was ready to get home. "Take us home, Bella. Take us home."

Chapter 15
The Storm Rolls Away

Emily's confidence grew now that everyone made it across the creek safely, including the cows. They had several miles left to go, but Emily was confident that she could make it home that night if the cattle didn't give her any problems. As long as Bella kept the cows headed home, Emily could relax.

"Well, Bella, you've turned into a regular old working horse. You deserve extra carrots tonight, and maybe two apples instead of one."

Taylor wholeheartedly agreed. "This is one amazing horse. I can't believe she found the cows and got us across this creek."

Momma cow and Oreo plodded along through the brush on the deer path. The wet earth still smelled fresh under Bella's feet. The sun was getting lower in the sky. Bella knew where she was going, and Emily knew Bella was going home. So Emily dropped the reins and started singing. She didn't care what Taylor thought. As Emily got to the pretty horses part, Taylor chimed in. They both sang together, knowing they had forged a new friendship out in the valley.

The Oregon sky put up a beautiful full moon while the sun was going down. As Emily, Taylor, Bella, and the cows walked out of the valley, Emily thought about the day's adventures. Emily thought about her horse and how special she was to her. The clouds were leaving the valley, and everything sparkled. Taylor was the first to speak. "Emily, thank you for helping me. I know I've never given you a reason to be my friend, but maybe sometime you would like to come ride with me? Or maybe I could come over here and we could ride into the valley again. Bella could teach Chance a thing or two."

"Oh my gosh, Taylor, what about Chance?" It was the first time she had thought about Taylor's horse since seeing Taylor on the stream bank.

"Oh, I'm not worried about him. He's probably been home for hours. But I wonder if my parents are out looking for me. If Chance did make it back, my parents are probably looking for my body right now." Taylor laughed a little to herself, covering up the nervousness she felt.

Emily was also getting nervous. By now, Emily had been gone longer than any other ride she ever took, and she was sure her parents were out looking for her. They rode for an hour or more with the cows in front of them. Emily got the feeling that they wanted to go home too.

Chapter 16
Almost Home

They came out of the trees onto a little dirt access road in the orchard. The sky was clear, and there was only some small gray puffy clouds left in the sky. The full moon was big and bright and the sun was going down behind the hills of the valley.

Emily was thankful that the moon was out and the storm clouds were gone. She was paying attention to the cows when she heard a very familiar voice calling her name.

"Emily! Emily!" Her father's voice was loud and clear in the dusky air.

"Dad! We're here on the road," Emily yelled back.

Emily, Taylor, Bella, Oreo, and the cows took up most of the width of the muddy road in the pear orchard. Emily could smell the ripening fruit and the grass and the muddy access road. She smiled a little to herself even though she knew she was in trouble. They walked around the bend in the road to find Emily's dad and Jason trotting toward them. "Young lady, you are in serious trouble when you get home."

Her dad's eyes widened with surprise at seeing the cows and Taylor with Emily. "Taylor Carey, what are you doing with Emily?"

Her dad looked at the new calf and had a look on his face that pleased Emily. Her dad's eyes softened and he released his clenched jaw. Emily knew her dad would be mad, but she also knew in the end his heart would be bursting with pride once she got the whole story out.

"Dad, I have so much to tell you about how Bella found the cows and how she helped us cross the creek."

Taylor chimed in, "If it wasn't for your daughter and Bella, Mr. Harris, I would still be out in the valley. I sprained my ankle pretty bad, and my horse ran off."

Bella's ears perked up at the sound of her name, and her step was a little lighter because they were going home. Emily could see the farmhouse in the distance and the little hill in Bella's pasture. She was happy because they did a good day's work. Emily had a new friend, and she was looking forward to her next adventure with her best friend Bella.